T0089055

PENGUIN CLASSICS

THE DISCOVERY OF AMERICA
BY THE TURKS

JORGE AMADO (1912–2001), the son of a cacao planter, was born in the Brazilian state of Bahia, which he would portray in more than twenty-five novels. His first novels, published when he was still a teenager, dramatize the class struggles of workers on Bahian cacao plantations. Amado was later exiled for his leftist politics, but his novels would always have a strong political perspective. Not until he returned to Brazil in the 1950s did he write his acclaimed novels *Gabriela, Clove and Cinnamon* and *Dona Flor and Her Two Husbands* (the basis for the successful film and Broadway musical of the same name), which display a lighter, more comic approach than his overtly political novels. One of the most renowned writers of the Latin American boom of the 1960s, Amado has had his work translated into more than forty-five languages.

GREGORY RABASSA (1922–2016) was a National Book Award–winning translator whose English-language versions of works by Gabriel García Márquez, Mario Vargas Llosa, Julio Cortázar, and Jorge Amado have become classics in their own right.

JOSÉ SARAMAGO (1922–2010) was a Nobel Prize–winning Portuguese writer. His many novels include *All the Names* and *Blindness*.

JORGE AMADO

The Discovery of
America by the Turks

Translated by
GREGORY RABASSA

Foreword by
JOSÉ SARAMAGO

PENGUIN BOOKS

PENGUIN BOOKS
Published by the Penguin Group
Penguin Group (USA) Inc., 375 Hudson Street, New York, New York 10014, U.S.A.
Penguin Group (Canada), 90 Eglinton Avenue East, Suite 700, Toronto, Ontario, Canada M4P 2Y3
(a division of Pearson Penguin Canada Inc.)
Penguin Books Ltd, 80 Strand, London WC2R 0RL, England
Penguin Ireland, 25 St Stephen's Green, Dublin 2, Ireland (a division of Penguin Books Ltd)
Penguin Group (Australia), 250 Camberwell Road, Camberwell, Victoria 3124, Australia
(a division of Pearson Australia Group Pty Ltd)
Penguin Books India Pvt Ltd, 11 Community Centre,
Panchsheel Park, New Delhi – 110 017, India
Penguin Group (NZ), 67 Apollo Drive, Rosedale, Auckland 0632, New Zealand
(a division of Pearson New Zealand Ltd)
Penguin Books (South Africa) (Pty) Ltd, 24 Sturdee Avenue,
Rosebank, Johannesburg 2196, South Africa

Penguin Books Ltd, Registered Offices:
80 Strand, London WC2R 0RL, England

First published in Penguin Books 2012

Published in Portuguese under the title *A descoberta da America pelos turcos* by Editora Record, Rio de Janeiro, 1994.

"A Certain Innocence" by José Saramago appears in this volume in a new translation by Gregory Rabassa. This selection is published in *The Notebook* by José Saramago, translated by Amanda Hopkinson and Daniel Hahn, Verso (London, 2010). Copyright © José Saramago and Editorial Caminho, SA, Lisbon, 2008-2010. Published by arrangement with Verso.

LIBRARY OF CONGRESS CATALOGING IN PUBLICATION DATA
Amado, Jorge, 1912-2001.
[Descoberta da América pelos turcos. English]
The discovery of America by the Turks / Jorge Amado ; translated from the Portuguese by Gregory Rabassa ; foreword by José Saramago.
p. cm.—(Penguin classics)
ISBN 978-0-14-310698-2
I. Rabassa, Gregory. II. Title.
PQ9697.A647D4713   2012   2012022549
869.3'41—dc23

Set in Sabon

ALWAYS LEARNING   PEARSON

146028962

Contents

Foreword

A Certain Innocence

For many years Jorge Amado tried and knew how to be the voice, the feeling, and the joy of Brazil. Few times will a writer succeed as well as he in becoming the mirror and the portrait of an entire people. An important part of the world of foreign readers came to know Brazil when they began to read Jorge Amado. And for many it was a surprise to discover in the books of Amado, along with the most transparent evidence, the complex heterogeneity, not only racial but also cultural, of Brazilian society. The generalized and stereotyped picture to which Brazil had been reduced, to the sum of white, black, mulatto, and Indian, was now being progressively corrected, albeit in an unequal way, by the dynamics of development in the multiple sectors and social activities of the country, and has received in the works of Amado a most solemn and at the same time delightful disavowal. We were not ignorant of the historic Portuguese immigration, nor, on a different scale and in different periods, of the German and Italian ones, but it was Amado who laid before our eyes how little we knew about it. The ethnic fan that cooled Brazil was much richer and more diversified than European perceptions had it, always contaminated by the selective habits of colonialism: After all, one had to include the multitude of Turks, Syrians, Lebanese, and *tutti quanti* who, beginning in the nineteenth century and continuing into the twentieth, almost right down to the present moment, left their countries of origin to turn themselves over, body and soul, to the seductions and also to the perils of the Brazilian El Dorado. And also so that Amado could open wide for them the doors of his books.

I take as an example of what I have been saying this small and delightful book, whose title, *The Discovery of America by the Turks*, is capable of immediately arousing the attention of the most apathetic of readers. Here will be told, in principle, the tale of two Turks—who, as Amado says, weren't Turks but were Arabs—Raduan Murad and Jamil Bichara, who had decided to immigrate to America for the conquest of wealth and women. It's not long, however, before the story that seemed to promise unity subdivides into other stories, in which dozens of characters are involved— violent men, whoremasters and tipplers, women as thirsty for sex as for domestic felicity; all of this in the district of Itabuna, Bahia, precisely where Amado (a coincidence?) happens to have been born. This Brazilian picaresque is no less violent than the Iberian ones. We are in the land of paid gunmen; cacao farms that were gold mines; fights decided by the stabs of a knife; colonels who exercised a lawless power, the origins of which no one is capable of understanding; and whorehouses where the whores were fought over like the purest of wives. These people think only of fornicating, of piling up money and lovers, and of drinking bouts. They are meat for Judgment Day, for eternal condemnation. Nevertheless, all through this turbulent story of evil counsel there breathes (to the reader's distress) a kind of innocence as natural as the wind that blows or the water that flows, as spontaneous as the grass that grows after a rainstorm. A wonder of the art of narration, *The Discovery of America by the Turks*, in spite of its almost schematic brevity and apparent simplicity, deserves a place beside the great novelistic murals such as *Jubiabá, Tent of Miracles*, and *The Violent Land*. It is said that you can recognize a giant by his finger. Here, then, is the giant's finger, the finger of Jorge Amado.

JOSÉ SARAMAGO

Preface

Roundabout the end of May 1991, I was in my house in Rio Vermelho, Bahia, when I got a phone call from Rome. The director of a public relations outfit was filling me in on a project and making me a proposition. An important Italian official had decided to commemorate the fifth centennial of the discovery of America with the publication of a book consisting of three stories by authors from the American continent: one in English by the American Norman Mailer, one in Spanish by the Mexican Carlos Fuentes, and one in Portuguese by me. The project called for the book to be published in four languages: Italian, English, Spanish, and Portuguese, three hundred thousand copies of which would be given out free to all passengers on flights between Italy and the three Americas on the various airlines between April and September 1992, the year of the fifth centennial.

The agency would acquire the rights for the texts of the three writers for a period of three years in the four languages. They asked me whether or not I might have some piece of a story tucked away somewhere of the anticipated length (they told me the number of bytes or such, and as I understand nothing about computers, I translated them into typewritten pages, seventy or so) and if I didn't have one whether I would consider writing one. They proposed a set amount in payment of author's rights. It seemed a bit low to me, so I hesitated and we agreed to discuss the matter further in July in Paris, where I would be traveling a month from then.

The idea was starting to grab me, so I gave it some thought. I remembered that when I was putting *Showdown* together I'd begun to think about an adventure (or misadventure) for the Arab Fadul, but I hadn't gotten around to writing it down. I didn't think it was needed for the structure of the novel. It was an amusing idea. I thought about it again and about bringing it to fruition.

I waited in Paris but the Italians never appeared, and I said to Zélia: "The mafiosi have disappeared. So much the better; now I can keep on working in peace on *Home Is the Sailor.*" I'd begun writing *Sailor* in Bahia. It so happened, however, that those guys contacted me again, came to Paris, accepted my price, and we signed a contract. I postponed writing the anti-memoirs and invented the novella you are about to read. In November of that year in Rome I turned in the manuscript, got my check, and began squandering the pittance.

At the same time I began selling the story in languages that had not been included in my contract with the agency. I signed agreements for translations into French, German, Russian, and Turkish. In September 1992 the French edition came out (Editions Stock) in a magnificent translation by Jean Orecchioni. The little book about the Turks was well received by the French critics and sold—and is still selling—quite well. It will appear in a pocket edition beginning next year. I must add that the Turkish edition, published early in 1993, is beautiful. As for the translation: I consider it perfect. Perfect translations are those in languages the author can't read.

The editions of the three stories in Italian, Portuguese, English, and Spanish in one volume should have been published in April 1992, but they weren't. They didn't become part of the commemorations of the fifth centennial, which had evidently degenerated, as anticipated, into a harsh and basic polemic: Epic or genocide? Discovery or conquest? Time passed, and I received no further news from the agency.

I didn't have any more news, but I did have my suspicions upon reading in the newspapers about "Operation Clean Hands," which had brought out into the open and put on trial the corruption of Italian political life—corruption that could be second only to the Brazilian variety—and included in its investigations a most important government establishment, whose directors had been brought to trial along with its president, who killed himself in jail. I was left scratching my head. I showed the report to Zélia: "I don't think those editions they planned on will ever reach the hands of passengers on the airlines; the project's gone down the drain."

Exactly. The agency that had drawn up the contract wrote to me immediately and told me the project had been abandoned, and they gave back to me the rights in the four languages in which they'd had the option. I phoned Carlos Fuentes to pass along the news, and he said he'd already sold the rights for publication in Spanish to a publisher in Madrid. I notified Sérgio Machado in Brazil: "The Turks have been set free. You can publish the book whenever you want."

If the reader of this little novella perceives a certain resemblance between the Arab Jamil Bichara, a character in the story, and Fadul Abdala, a character in a previous novel; between Raduan Murad and Fuad Karam; between the village of Itaguassu and the place called Tocaia Grande, he mustn't think it a simple coincidence. It's just more proof of the fact that I'm a limited and repetitive novelist, according to the line of the current and express opinion of the noble gentlemen of national criticism—an opinion that is mentioned and repeated here in writing in order to comply with same.

Otherwise, everything's just fine. I hope readers will have some fun with the events and incidents leading to Adma's nuptials, which took place in the city of Itabuna at the beginning of cacao culture, in the early years of the century, when the Turks finally discovered America, landed in Brazil, and became Brazilians of the best kind.

JORGE AMADO

For Zélia
in the joys and sadnesses of this autumn.

For António Alçada Baptista and
Nuno Lima de Carvalho,
who discovered Brazil and
conquered the heathens with
the weapons of devotion
and friendship.

It's time now for us to discover America—said the prophet Tawil—we're a bit late and we're losing money.

—From the secret archives, a volume of
The Minor Prophets

A divine inspiration, a masterwork of the Lord, a great gift, a delectable pussy, a twat worthy of an Angel.

—The book of Genesis, chapter [on Perfection]

The Discovery of America by the Turks

or

How the Arab Jamil Bichara,

Tamer of Forests,

On a Visit to the City

of Itabuna,

Seeking Nourishment

For His Body,

Was There Offered

Fortune and Marriage;

Or Yet Again

the Nuptials of Adma

I

If we are to believe Iberian historians, be they Spanish or
Portuguese, the discovery of the Americas by the Turks, who
are not Turks at all but Arabs of good stock, came about
after a long delay, in relatively recent times, during the past
century and not before.
We must bear in mind that being interested parties, the
Peninsular chroniclers are suspect. All they were interested
in doing was praising and puffing up the deeds and figures
of Spaniards and Portuguese, of Christopher Columbus,
Amerigo Vespucci, Vasco da Gama, Ferdinand Magellan,
and other bigwigs; Castilians and Lusitanians of the highest
order, of the noblest Christian lineage, of the purest blood;
fearless, indomitable heroes. To begin our conversation it is
worth noting that, armed with birth certificates and testimonials, Italian publicists have, in their woppish way,
claimed for the other peninsula the glory of being the cradle
of Columbus and Vespucci: the one who discovered and the
one who took advantage of it and labeled the unknown lands
with his name. The Spaniards parry with other papers, other
testimonials, so who'll ever know who's right? Certificates
have been falsified; testimonials have been bought with the
vile metal. If the Spaniards deserve little credit, the Italians
deserve even less, as is easily shown by Vespucci's fraud. And
what have they to say about the Vikings? The Discovery is
all a great mélange.
    In the immigrant ship bringing them from the Middle
East, from the mountains of Syria and Lebanon to the virgin forests of Brazil, a difficult and stormy passage, Raduan

Murad, a fugitive from justice for vagrancy and gambling, a scholar with seductive prose, revealed to his steerage companion, the Syrian Jamil Bichara, that during sleepless nights bent over beat-up old books about Columbus's first voyage, in the roll of sailors making up the crew of one of the three caravels on that festive excursion, he'd discovered the name of a certain Alonso Bichara. Bichara the Moor, signed on maybe, who knows, by a press gang, one of those many heroes forgotten when it was time for celebrations and rewards: The admiral is covered with glory and the crew is covered with shit (in spite of all his erudition, Raduan Murad had a foul mouth).

The truth, or a bunch of bootlegged goods? Raduan Murad was imaginative, inventive, and as far as scruples were concerned, he cultivated none at all. A few years later, settled in the virgin lands now, he would invent the "Itabuna ploy," done with three unlike cards and something new at the poker table, something quite useful in bluffing and whose fame spread far and wide in the southern region of Bahia. Truth or trick? Of no great concern because the events to be recounted here took place with Jamil as their protagonist, and not with his purported forebear, Moorish from the Bichara, Spanish from the Alonso, of doubtful existence. It is better to concern ourselves with proven, undeniable facts, even though the truthful story does touch upon the miraculous.

The reference to the discovery of America comes from the current and omnipresent celebrations: A peaceable person can't take the smallest step or blow the slightest fart without the Fifth Centenary landing on his head. Of the Discovery, say the descendants of the fearless men who discovered the other side of the sea; of the Conquest, exclaim the descendants of the massacred Indians; of the enslaved blacks, cultures wiped out by the passage of mercenaries and missionaries carrying the cross of Christ and the baptismal font.

The argument is all laid on, a violent polemic with no middle ground, no agreement in sight, sectarianism predominating on both sides, and anyone who wants to can get involved and leave himself open to carrying off the scraps. I'm not going to be the one to do it, no not I, a Brazilian of mixed blood, the fruit of the Discovery and of the Conquest, of the mixture. I am only recounting here what happened to Jamil Bichara, Raduan Murad, and other Arabs in full discovery of Brazil back there at the beginning of the century. The first to arrive from the Middle East carried papers issued by the Ottoman Empire, which is why right down to the present moment they're all stamped as Turks, making up that fine Turkish nation, one of the many in the amalgamation that has composed and is still composing the Brazilian nation.

The ship that the young Jamil Bichara and the wise Raduan Murad had boarded made port in the Bay of All Saints in October 1903, 411 years after the epic of Columbus's caravels. But this did not cause their landing not to be a discovery and a conquest, for the lands to the south in the state of Bahia, where they set themselves up to do battle, were at the time covered with virgin forest. The planting of crops and the building of houses was just beginning. Colonels and their hired guns were killing one another in disputes over land, the best in the world for growing cacao. Coming from different regions were backlanders, Sergipeans, Jews, Turks—they were called Turks, those Arabs, Syrians, and Lebanese—all of them Brazilians.

2

Begun on board, the friendship that linked Jamil Bichara and Raduan Murad continued and grew stronger when the two immigrants decided without any previous discussion to test their lives in the southern lands of Bahia, the newly discovered El Dorado of cacao.

During their dismal crossing Jamil had come to admire the wisdom and skills of Murad. Almost a child still, a youth, Jamil filled with enthusiasm as he watched his traveling companion overcome seasickness and squander his knowledge and cunning at the poker table—just a plank that went up and down with the rolling of the ship—and the backgammon board. Or as he listened to him declaim love poetry, some of it of a delightful concupiscence, about odalisques and wine, which he recited in Arabic or Persian on moonlit nights under a blanket of stars spread out over the sea. Jamil and the others who listened, a coarse rabble, didn't know the Persian tongue, nor did the ancient name of Omar Khayyám mean anything to them, but the sonority of the stanzas of the Rubaiyat, the enveloping melody alleviated the harshness of the voyage and served to increase Raduan Murad's prestige. He disembarked surrounded by respect, his pockets garnished with coins of copper, silver, and gold, earnings brought him by talent and manual skill.

The El Dorado of cacao! People were hurrying there from the backlands, from the northeastern states—Sergipe, the smallest of them, the closest and the poorest, saw itself become almost depopulated of men; they were abandoning

wives, fiancées, lovers. The Arabs, too: No sooner did they
get off the vessel of the Bahia Shipping Line at the port of
Ilhéus than they made for the forests, going off in search
of a sure and easy fortune. Easy fortune? Better to say an
uncertain and risky fortune. If the chosen one didn't start
off by kicking the bucket in his first encounter with thugs,
if he persisted, it would take a lot of heart and hard work
for the courage to face death.

Jamil was well-disposed for work and was fearless by he-
redity. A Levantine born in the tribal lands of the Euphrates,
he had inherited the valor of tribes that fought among themselves just for the fun of fighting and for the pleasure of
life. Something similar might be said about Raduan Murad,
in spite of all the gossip. Without even making note of his
moral courage, which was questionable, how could anyone
deny the boldness and lack of fear in someone who more
than once had stood up to toughs in gambling dens, unarmed,
too, in a land where no one went about without his shotgun
or his pistol? Calm, serene, impassive, even when suspicions
and threats were forthcoming (truculent people didn't
always greet the "Itabuna ploy" with laughter or applause).

As for saying, as some did, that he was a sworn enemy of
work, holding it in a holy horror, as so frequently happens
with educated people, it would be a matter of an obvious
injustice and ill will. If, in fact, during his early youth the
Professor—that was what many people respectfully called
him—stubbornly avoided tasks that were not in line with
his intellectual capacity, there was no more assiduous and
punctual laborer at the poker table or in any other game
of chance. Chance? For Raduan Murad there was no such
thing as a game of chance. In a round of conversation he was
unbeatable, and from time to time, as a pastime, he would
write in fluent Portuguese, with a captivating Oriental accent,
newspaper articles about problems of the cacao zone. The
only reason he didn't write them more frequently was
that there weren't enough newspapers to publish them and
he feared they might want to make him schoolmaster or

appoint him to a government position. Inclined to preserve his freedom, he loved above all else his right to make use of his time. He didn't want it to be ruled by the hands of a clock.

Although they were different from each other in everything, the two Turks, the Syrian and the Lebanese, forged a friendship that nothing could disturb. They were like brothers, even though of enemy nationalities. Jamil had been born Syrian, while Raduan was Lebanese by birth and by conviction. Nor did they coincide in matters of religion, young Jamil swearing by Allah and Mohammed, and the skeptic Raduan, while born to a Christian family of the Maronite sect, had been converted by life's experiences and the vice of books into a materialist (more or less immoral). And the difference in age was no obstacle to their comradeship. When all this was taking place, Jamil had yet to celebrate his thirtieth birthday, a randy stud vied for by ladies of the night. Raduan was past forty and a charmer in his fifties, the wonder of all the girls, large and small.

Nor did it matter that Itaguassu, a hamlet lost in the woods where Jamil toiled, was quite a distance from Itabuna, a growing and prosperous city to which Raduan had conceded the privilege of his living and operating. Once a month Jamil would come to Itabuna with the intention of renewing the supplies for his place of business, tiny but the only one in Itaguassu, where he sold a bit of everything to the small population of the village and the vast flow of those passing through: herdsmen, hired hands, gunmen, and the wandering nation of whores that came and went through the cacao clearings. He would also come unexpectedly to relieve his boredom and have another look at civilization—"Are you here for your bath of civilization, old chum?" Raduan would greet him when he saw him arrive without notice—to have some fun, relax (nobody's made of iron) in the cabaret, bars, a whorehouse. It was his feast day. Jamil and Raduan, the philosopher, never separated, gabbing endlessly, lots of laughs, drinks, polkas, and mazurkas. On nights of great

merriment, on the streets of Itabuna, arm in arm with
Cockeye Paula or some other woman, Raduan would get
the urge to declaim in Arabic love poems in which the wine
flowed and sultanas danced. Holding hands with Glorinha
Goldass as he listened, Jamil was moved to tears.

3

Sitting and resting at the end of the day's hustle and bustle—
oh, so tired!—on the sidewalk by the Itaguassu Emporium, in
front of the establishment, his living quarters in the rear, sev-
eral years after the engagement ceremony, Jamil Bichara
laughed loud and hard as he remembered the problems of
the deal concerning the small dry-goods store and the danger he had subjected himself to when, advised by Raduan
Murad, Ibrahim Jafet had offered him a partnership in the
Bargain Shop as compensation for the hand in marriage of
Adma, his oldest daughter. The three younger girls were
married, for better or worse, but she, cherry intact, sour,
crabby, undamaged, more than merely a virgin: an old maid.

Because of her (and because of the store, a good deal!)
Jamil had been in danger of abandoning Itaguassu and his
newly established Emporium—prestigious in name only—
where he sold flour and beans, cachaça, and sandals. Later
on he got to selling both wholesale and retail, supplying the
plantations in the region and the inhabitants of the village
with a varied stock that went from jerked beef to denim
pants, from raw-leather sandals to ladies' hats and boots,
bolts of cloth, spools of linen, needles, hair oil, pictures of
Catholic saints and miracle workers. Although a good Muslim of the Shiite sect, Jamil had no religious prejudices when
it came to making money. Allah is great, his wisdom is infinite, he can read men's hearts, he understands and esteems
everything.

The Bicharas, numerous and enterprising, were scattered all through the ports of the Mediterranean and its

adjacencies. They were established in Spain, as has already been noted, in Crete, in Egypt, and in Morocco, going from Libya to Italy, reaching Senegal. A certain Michel Bichara had headed a band of footpads in the French city of Marseilles, ending up on the guillotine. The first to discover America, heading for Brazil, was Jamil. In the annals of the family his name appears next to that of Michel, the brigand of the port city.

On the day of his departure, before sailing, he went to kneel in front of Mullah Tahar Bichara, his great-uncle, a wise and holy man, a favored disciple of the Prophet, who spoke with Allah during moments of prayer. It was predicted he would soon attain the honors and emoluments of an aya-tollah. From him Jamil got a letter of recommendation addressed to their countryman Anuar, sheikh of the tribe of the Marons, who was well established with cacao planta-tions in the state of Bahia. A letter to the moneybags and prayers to Allah, who would not abandon his son lost in the vastness of America. The mullah would see to it that the name of Jamil would remain in the mouth and ears of Allah and of his prophet Mohammed.

The letter was indeed valuable, determining for Jamil the choice of the region of southern Bahia. There he had some-one to lean on as he began life. Surely the requests of the venerable Tahar would make it possible for the new Brazil-ian not to feel lost, abandoned in his adopted country, which he must conquer foot by foot and day by day. It is incumbent upon Allah to assist his children at decisive moments, defend them against the temptations of Shaitan, the insidious Satan, point out the right path to them, stop them from committing a great error capable of making them suf-fer on earth the horrors of hell.

Allah accompanied Jamil's steps as his wandering son for a long time when, for the Turk Anuar Maron, he covered the whole cacao region from north to south and east to west as the borders grew longer and the distances greater and greater. He saved him from multiple dangers: rattlesnakes and jararacussu vipers and their deadly fangs, the endemic smallpox, black pox, which was certain death, ambushes, gunmen, the conflicts and battles of colonel against colonel, in which killers and henchmen left bodies on the road marked by carbine and stab wounds.

Anuar Maron—Colonel Maron, because he was a millionaire plantation owner with some eighty thousand tons—added to his harvest the meager pickings of those who owned just a small piece of cultivated land and were without means to transport their dry cacao to the warehouses of the export firms established in Ilhéus and Itabuna. Jamil gathered up the production of the small farmers for him, in an agreement with representatives of Colonel Misael Tavares, the cacao king, or Colonel Basílio de Oliveira, the master of Pirangi.

For four years, riding mules and donkeys or on foot along dangerous bypaths, Jamil swept through the forest and conquered it as he bought cacao at low prices. He learned how to dicker and to practice accounting and medicine, establishing relationships and friendships, as godfather baptizing children into the Catholic faith—may Allah understand and forgive him.

Allah understood all and forgave everything; he kept watch over him, attentive to the mullah's prayers. Jamil had proof of this when a dispute separated him once and for all from Colonel Anuar Maron. In the village of Ferradas, where he'd been sent on an errand, he met and gathered to his bosom the capricious Jove, a wild and lusty half-breed. The affair caused talk, and news of it reached the colonel's ears. Anuar Maron had set up a house for Jove, had taken her out of the red-light district, wanted her all for himself and wouldn't hear of anyone else grazing in his pastures. He settled accounts with his countryman and fired him. He didn't send a gunman who was a good shot to lie in wait for the bold fellow in an ambush and send him off to the land of the stiffs. It must have been because he remembered the mullah and had a great deal of respect for him.

On that occasion, when Jamil saw himself in a hole, out of work and with no place to turn, Colonel Noberto de Faria made him a proposition. A plantation owner even richer than the Turk Maron, the owner of leagues of land planted haphazardly and not too great a distance from Itaguassu, he'd developed a friendship with Jamil, whom he'd come to know in the whorehouses of Itabuna, of which he was an assiduous and jolly frequenter. Desirous of seeing prosper the settlement that had sprung up near his lands, Colonel Noberto, when he heard of Jamil's troubles, asked him if he might not be interested in going into business in Itaguassu, dealing on his own instead of working for a boss. What else could Jamil be longing for from life? It was his dream, but where was the capital to start it? Noberto de Faria, a native of Sergipe with traces of mulatto, a man of honor and vision, placed the necessary sum at Jamil's disposal, trusting in him and swearing to the great esteem in which he held him. He called him his partner at table and in bed, because they had the same girls, ate from the same plate, and had similar tastes: small boobs, big asses, tight twats. Pleasant concordances always reinforce the bonds of friendship.

He set himself up under the protection of Allah—Allah is great—and Mohammed is his prophet, it's worth repeating—with dough loaned by Colonel Noberto de Faria. Three years later he'd already paid back the loan and was enlarging the Emporium bit by bit. It was still a long way off from being compared with the shops and stores in the cities of Ilhéus and Itabuna or the villages of Ferradas, Olivença, Agua Preta, and Pirangi, but it wouldn't be long (and who could doubt it?) before Itaguassu would cease to be just a settlement and the Emporium would be head and shoulders, as far as stock and clientele were concerned, over Ibrahim Jafet's Bargain Shop. Jamil Bichara, sitting on the sidewalk in front of his business, thanked Allah for having saved him when, taken by greed, haste, and the temptation of easy money, he had almost followed the advice of Shaitan: to abandon Itaguassu, marry Adma, and ruin himself.

4

The events took place when Ibrahim Jafet began to see that things were in bad shape. The prospects for the store's balance sheet were dismal: With his son-in-law Alfeu behind the counter and at the cash register, the winds of bankruptcy began to blow. Dark were the forecasts for daily life at home: Adma, condemned to spinsterhood, had assumed command of the house and family with a harsh zeal as storm clouds threatened the dwindling moments of pleasure. The economic situation and his pleasant life were in imminent danger.

The Bargain Shop, a small dry-goods store with plenty of customers, a good inventory, and credit in the marketplace, had been enough to serve for many years the family's needs and the owner's modest pleasures of fishing, checkers, and backgammon. The uncontested head of the tribe during her life, Sálua, Ibrahim's wife, had taken charge and busied herself with the store: The notions counter saw prosperous times and brought in good savings. A handsome, sturdy woman with languid eyes that looked like those on a calendar print, she was the disciplinarian, stern, demanding and yet gentle, tender, and affable as well.

An expert at marking prices and finding bargains, she did a little cheating as she manipulated the yardstick and the shears, laughing and gossiping with the customers, almost all women. Esteemed, respected, with a light hand in a caress and a heavy one in punishment, Sálua ran the shop, her daughters, and her husband with fine competence.

The intellectual Raduan Murad, a persona most grata

and a good friend of the family, Ibrahim's companion at checkers and backgammon, proclaimed her the matriarch. Strict and moral, she was no less capable of love in dealing with her daughters or restraint when in bed with her idolized husband, to whom she consented in all things— consented or commanded? She would kill herself working so that he might have a morning of fishing, an afternoon of siesta and gambling, content to have him at night: every night, starting at nine o'clock, the time for putting out the lamp and lighting up her huge sultana eyes for their unflagging nuptials in the darkness of the bedroom.

Matriarchs are like that: imposing and demanding with ordinary people, liberal and magnanimous with their favorites. Raduan Murad would explain that to his admirers gathered to listen to him at the poker table, at a bar, in a cabaret, in brothels—locales where he squandered wisdom and buffoonery. He would cite the example of Ibrahim Jafet: a unique and exclusive favorite, a regular lord!

Sálua's unexpected death changed the ways at home and in the store. Disoriented, Ibrahim added the nighttime frequenting of whores to his morning fishing and his afternoon checkerboard, in search of compensation and consolation. One today, another tomorrow, the girls only served to keep him far away from the bedroom in the living quarters above the store, which had become cold and gloomy ever since his beloved had left him. Even if he could have managed to blend together with one stroke of magic the eminent partners, the ablest specialists at their trade in a medley of techniques and styles and in one single dissolute bed, not even then would it have matched the renowned mastery, the universal wisdom of Sálua. A divine gift, most certainly, Murad stated, because there was no place where she could have learned it or anyone who could have taught her. Sálua's bed, nevermore!

5

The girls took their mother's place behind the counter, but they were less concerned with the merchandise or the customers than with their gentleman friends. With the brakes off now they did whatever they wanted to. In Sálua's time they would wave to boys from the upper windows of the house, that chaste mongrel type of lovemaking; with their mother gone there was smooching behind the counter, kisses and touches at the backyard gate. With the exception of Adma, who didn't like selling and hadn't found anyone who would court her. There was skimping on the younger daughters' trousseaus. They married boys from the region. None of them chose a fellow countryman with a propensity or disposition for business. There were expressions of praise for the marriage of Jamile, the second in age, because Ranulfo Pereira, the groom, was well on his way, with planted fields in Mutuns and his four thousand tons of cacao already harvested. Samira, two years younger, was following a modest but worthy destiny as she received her nuptial blessings in partnership with the telegrapher Clóvis Esmeraldino. Although not a lad of many possessions, he was good with words, a riddler, a decipherer of word games, and a versifier for calendars, with funds from some dubious income, and a man of some luster and esteem. As for the youngest, Fárida, she was said to be the prettiest of the Turk girls in that store—tidbit, to use the covetous term of Alfeu Bandeira, a tailor's apprentice who worked under the watchful eye of Master Ataliba Reis, owner of the English Haberdashery, whose doors opened across the street from the home of the

Jafets. To tell the truth, Alfeu wasn't pleased with the way the tidbit would offer herself with a brazenness that was firmly condemned by the families in the neighborhood. All that necking and so much petting was bound to come to a bad end. It came to a good one, however, with a hasty marriage. Fine silk veils fluttered over Fárida's intrepid little belly, four months pregnant, with orange blossoms, the symbols of purity and virginity, on her wreath. "A virgin only in her armpits," was the comment of Master Ataliba, chosen as godfather by the groom. "In the armpits, you think?" doubted Raduan Murad, godfather of the bride, skeptical, as a learned man should be. Both of them, however, were in accord with Dona Abigail Carvalho, the seamstress responsible for the bride's dress, as that distinguished lady compared her to a cherub.

Without any cacao or word puzzles, Alfeu struggled behind the counter of the Bargain Shop. He wasn't lacking in goodwill, but he was in everything else. When the time came to balance the books it was pandemonium. When Ibrahim woke up to the fact, he saw his fishing, his betting on checkers and backgammon, his nights of a spree, and the solvency of his business all threatened. The blame for the calamity didn't lie completely with Alfeu, because at that very same time Adma had gone on the warpath.

It was a holy war. She had persevered in it ever since Sálua's soul had appeared to her in a dream, suffering in the infinite and unable to assume her deserved place in the hand of the Eternal Father because of the dissipation into which the family had fallen after they took her to the cemetery. How could she enjoy the delights of good fortune if on earth her loved ones were living in iniquity and sin? In order to save the soul of her mother, Adma had entered into battle.

She set goals for herself, established during her sleepless nights of solitude and unhappiness. There was little she could do with regard to Jamile's arrogant behavior, however, as her sister began to take on the airs of a rich lady, quite stuck on herself. She was drinking coffee and belching up chocolate, and there was little Adma could do about it, or with the sassy Samira, a scoffer and joker in the eyes of her husband and a shameless hussy in the mouths of everyone else. One lived in Mutuns and the other next door to the train station, both far from her immediate authority. Only on the rare occasions when the wicked girls came to visit did Adma bare her breast and vent her feelings. Jamile would respond with disdain; Samira would laugh in her face and mock her.

She was, on the other hand, able to do quite a bit in the case of Fárida, Alfeu, and Ibrahim, there at hand and with no escape. She allowed them none. She put the house in order and demanded decorum in their habits. She obliged Fárida, poor cherub, to abandon her happy life and come help with the household chores—so many and so tedious!—starting with the care of her son (bottles, dirty diapers, wet clothes, crying, doo-doo, and vomit) instead of continuing her shameless behavior with Alfeu, exchanging kisses over the counter, pinches and pats in front of customers, as though they were still courting. It hadn't been she, Adma, who'd wiggled her body at the garden gate, so why should she have to take care of the baby's piss and shit?

But the main target of her challenge was Ibrahim, to rescue him from the disorder and perdition in which he had been wallowing from the beginning of his widowerhood, when he abandoned family matters completely. If Adma could bring him back to the righteous path, Sálua's soul could finally reach paradise. It was a holy mission, and she set about bringing it off, no matter what the cost.

From Sálua Adma had inherited her strong character, her sternness, and her talent for command. It was a pity she hadn't inherited her facial features or her figure. In those particulars she took after her father, rawboned and without the abundant breasts or hips, the sway in her walk, the large eyes, or the silken hair of her mother and sisters. The slight fuzz they all had on their upper lip, one more mark of beauty, in Adma's case had grown into a thick mustache. Who is to blame for the injustices of heaven?

With age and dejection, the moral gifts she had inherited

from Sálua had turned into aggressiveness and intolerance. Raduan Murad, a student of human nature and cause and effect, didn't call her a matriarch; lowering his voice, the worthy man declared her: a virago!

Examining the various facets of his problems during his threatened mornings of fishing, Ibrahim came to the conclusion that there was only one single outstanding solution capable of resolving the moral and financial crisis and freeing him simultaneously from the ineptitude of his son-in-law and the despotism of his oldest daughter—the others were delights, all three of them. He had to find some fellow countryman who was single and of small means to take over the management of the Bargain Shop and take Adma as his wife. The suitor's Arab blood would be a guarantee of his vocation for business and readiness for work. His modest condition would facilitate bringing off the wedding. If it didn't work out that way, how was he going to face up to ugliness instead of beauty and sourness in place of propriety?

Everybody knows, and it's stated in books, that a woman's true beauty doesn't lie in her physical charms, nor do they come first. The true beauty of a woman rests, before anything else, in the virtues that adorn her heart and beautify her soul. Keeping in mind her undeniable and extraordinary virtues—her status of heiress, partnership in the profits of the store, and her spotless virginity—how could anyone say that Adma wasn't beautiful?

Besides that, she wasn't a show-off like her sister or crippled or weak in the head. Absolute purity, outstanding: She'd never known a suitor's boldness, never watched the moon rise by the garden gate. With Adma decked out with lace and ribbons, and the profits from the Bargain Shop, who knows whether he might just find a candidate capable of leading her to the altar and doing him that great favor?

A difficult task, Ibrahim concluded, but a necessary, urgent, and vital one: Adma had reached the age of sourness and evil.

6

At the bar, Ibrahim sought out Raduan Murad's advice and opinion over the backgammon board. He found an enthusiastic reception for his idea and concrete help for the success of the plan.

"You can count on me, friend Ibrahim. We'll set out together in this hunt for the rara avis. Let's begin by analyzing the matter in depth."

That lark would be a gift from heaven, something tailormade for filling idle time in that newly born city, so devoid of entertainment. Outside of gambling, the bar, the cabaret, and girlie houses, there was nothing to do. Caught up by his comrade's story, Raduan Murad half-closed his eyes, content with life. He disagreed only with the concept of beauty put forth by Ibrahim, not denying, however, its standing as a commonplace taken from treatises on morality.

"Moral treatises, monuments of hypocrisy! Virtue might be excellent for getting into heaven after you're dead, but in bed, my dear Ibrahim, what matters is the flesh, what is properly called 'matter.'"

Putting the pieces into play, they had all of their countrymen in Itabuna pass in review. A lot of them, all welldisposed toward work, some of proven seriousness. One of the bachelors, Adib, the youngest of three brothers, orphaned on both sides, happened to be a waiter right there in that bar. Cheerful and sure of himself, he was manifestly expert in collecting money and making change, which was a prime indication. The bad part was his age. He was too young for Adma.

"Adma's already past thirty," Ibrahim confessed.

Raduan pushed that objection aside, however. A difference in age means little or nothing in the success of a marriage. What a young lad starting out in life needs beside him is a judicious wife who can show him the way. In a marriage between an old man and a young woman the husband runs the risk of cuckoldry, but in the opposite situation there's nothing to fear. A woman doesn't grow horns, isn't that so? An irrefutable argument.

Determined not to waste any time, they immediately set about with their soundings. Didn't Adib feel like getting married, having a home, a nice home, a wife and children? Surprised at the question, the waiter thought a bit before answering that right now he had no wish to get married, no sir. Not yet twenty, he felt too young to tie himself down. Especially under those circumstances, because he was head over heels in love with Procópia.

"Procópia?" Raduan became interested. "The civil judge's woman?"

Adib smacked his lips with an obscene sound of satisfaction.

"The very same, yes, sir."

This was news of little bearing, even though it was of interest. An encyclopedia of urban and rural life, Raduan Murad kept abreast of everything that went on in Itabuna and its surroundings, including apparently irrelevant facts. An incomparable well of information, if he didn't know a detail of some intrigue, he would invent it, and it so happened that most of the time he was right. When required he would foresee the course of events, leaving his audience dumbfounded. Life, after all, was nothing but a game of poker: All you had to do was substitute events and people for the cards and chips. In either case, at the gambling table or in the lottery of life, Raduan wasn't averse to bluffing; quite the opposite. He wasn't infallible, but he didn't miss very often. He gave a deep sigh as he remembered Procópia's breasts. She was crazy mad.

"Congratulations, lad, but watch out for the judge.

Dr. Gracindo is like a feudal lord. If he gets an inkling of that illicit agreement he'll put you in jail and take a scabbard to you to teach you some respect for somebody else's woman."

They were ready to consider Adib a cast-off card when they heard that surprised individual laugh and say, "I can tell you, though, that if the daughter of some plantation owner loaded down with dough should show up on my doorstep, I wouldn't tell her to get lost. . . ."

The friends exchanged glances: cacao farm or commercial establishment; very little difference. Adib remained inscribed on the list of candidates, the only one up till now. They'd have another chat with him if Ibrahim couldn't find a better prospect in Ilhéus.

7

An inspiration came to Raduan Murad as he moved his pieces with scant attention and, interrupting a move, patted his partner on the shoulder and announced, "Great news, my friend Ibrahim. I've found the man we're looking for. Ideal as both a partner and a son-in-law. It came to me just now. His name is Jamil Bichara. Do you know him?"

Ibrahim knew who he was. He knew him by sight and had heard of him. A fellow countryman with a huge build and a powerful voice. Glorinha Goldass, that adorable plague of a woman, never let his name leave her delicious lips: It was Jamil here, Jamil there; she'd tell funny stories and mourn the fellow's prolonged absence. He'd disappeared lately from the streets of Itabuna, where he was missed.

"He stopped working for Anuar Maron," Raduan explained, "and he opened a business in one of those depots lost out in the woods. Where, I don't know. He told me the name, but I've forgotten it. Glorinha's the one who should know. When he shows up here he never goes to a hotel; he sets himself up in her room just like he was a plantation owner with a two-ton crop and the hooker was part of his account."

Raduan couldn't add much more concerning the whereabouts and the plans of the Sultan (he'd given Jamil that nickname because his fellow countryman was so crazy about women). The last time he'd seen him was quite awhile ago, precisely in that same bar and in the company of Glorinha Goldass. He was complaining about his heavy workload and

the awful quality of the whores in that end of the earth
where he'd got himself stuck. If all those problems were still
there, then Jamil would certainly be open to Ibrahim's proposition. Raduan didn't know of anyone else so well-disposed
to work and eager to make money. As a partner, perfect. As
a son-in-law, all they had to know was whether Jamil would
accept the challenge.

"Because, just between us, my friend Ibrahim, our dear
Adma . . . I can't deny her virtues—I'm a sinner; I don't
understand those things. But her looks . . ."

"I know, old man. She took after me. It was her misfortune."

Talk was of no use because the indicated party wasn't
around to discuss the commercial status, balance, and
promissory notes, or concepts of beauty and physical and
moral values. He'd disappeared with no indication of when
he might return to Itabuna. Still, Raduan advised Ibrahim
to be patient. But that proposal was turned down immediately. No, old friend, he couldn't wait another day for that
crisis to be resolved, before his son-in-law Alfeu and the
cherub made a complete shambles of the store, before his
daughter Adma—daughter? governess, a marabout!—took
complete control, reducing him to the status of a slave, a
eunuch.

With tears in his eyes and in a tremulous, stammering
voice, Ibrahim opened the last floodgates of shame, abandoning any trace of self-respect. He laid out the horrors of
his tragedy:

"My dear friend Raduan. I'm going to confess everything to you, the disgrace that's overtaken me. My daughter
Adma's virtues are to blame. . . ."

"I never trusted them. . . . Virtue is so sad and bossy."
Avid to learn the details of this story, Raduan encouraged
the confidences. "Don't be ashamed, Ibrahim; open up your
heart. We're like family."

Ready to chain him to the counter all morning and afternoon, to condemn him to abstinence at night besides, Adma
was turning her father's life into a hell, every day more

tyrannical and violent. "An implacable fury, my friend."
Scandal upon scandal, to the delight of the neighborhood.
On his mornings for fishing she would accuse him of indo-
lence and of abandoning the business to go off and lounge
by the river; of irresponsibility in the afternoon during his
siestas in the hammock strung up in the yard between two
trees, and his time for bar and backgammon. It got even
worse at night, when, right after dinner, he would leave to
have a little fun. Tearing her hair, screaming, Adma would
shout to high heaven. People would cluster in the street listening to her. In the early morning she'd wait for him,
clutching four stones in her hands. That's how it was. . . .

"I know quite well, Ibrahim. I was a witness. I'll never
forget."

Ibrahim felt his capacity for resistance diminishing, his
soul weakening. He'd reduced his daily fishing to twice a
week, shortened his siestas, worked harder in the store. It
was the life of a black slave, a sad affair. But there were
worse things, much worse.

"I have to tell you everything, my friend! It isn't just my
character I'm losing. . . ." He lowered his voice and his eyes.
"My hard-on, too. . . ."

"Hard-on, Ibrahim? How can that be possible?"

"Witchcraft!" In the end he'd become the victim of some
fearsome witchcraft. It had happened when he was all tight
into a whore and, all of a sudden, during the best part of his
goody-gooey, he heard Adma's evil voice and in the darkness caught sight of her grim face, and he immediately went
limp, right then and there. That wasn't the end of it. The
curse persisted for the rest of the night. It was of no avail for
the whore to make any effort; there was no trick capable of
getting his dick up.

"She's gelding me, Raduan, my friend."

"It's more serious than I thought, Ibrahim. We really
can't wait for Jamil Bichara or whoever it's going to be. You
go to Ilhéus right away, tomorrow, while I go have a talk
with Adib. The way things stand, in a little while not even
marriage will save our Adma."

At the very moment when Ibrahim was confiding his miseries to his friend and counselor, an extraordinary coincidence was taking place, one worthy of inclusion in this faithful account of Adma's nuptials, in which coincidences and magical moments keep running into each other. In that peaceful late afternoon, having dropped off his suitcase in Glorinha Goldass's room and taken a bath to rid himself of the dust of his trip, Jamil Bichara was all prepared to give his body some nourishment, which was why he'd come to Itabuna. To replenish the stock of the Emporium and to feed his little dovey-doo, to dance at the cabaret, bat the breeze with Raduan Murad, attending to the necessities of both body and spirit.

None of the characters gathered at the bar, at the whorehouse, on the upper floor of the living quarters could have guessed that all that talking and activity was part of the scheme put together by Shaitan, the Islamic devil. On his chessboard lay the fate of Jamil and, in the bargain, the souls of the other figures.

8

While Jamil Bichara, in Glorinha Goldass's room at Afonsina's happy house, was giving abundant and varied nourishment to his dovey-doo, while Ibrahim Jafet, bent down under the weight of his shame, was deciding to dine at home and confront the wrath of his daughter Adma, Raduan Murad, at a table in Sante's bar, empty of customers at that hour, was reflecting on the catastrophic situation in which his old friend and companion found himself.

Man's fortune is fickle, the saying goes, and Ibrahim's example proves it twice over. Only a few years ago a prosperous merchant, a respected family man with lots of leisure at his disposal, the husband of the most competent, desirable, and virtuous of women, he had suddenly been transformed into that thing we now see. From being the exclusive favorite of the matriarch Sálua—a pasha he was!—he was on the point of becoming impecunious and impotent. In a toast to Sálua, Raduan Murad sipped his raki, emptying the glass.

Raduan kept no set schedule for lunch or dinner (except when he was invited), nor for sleeping. That he would do during breaks from his elegant prose, his art, and from the poker table, his main profession, from the books he read and reread, from the pieces in checkers and backgammon games, from sprees with his hookers, his innocent diversions. In exchange for that, he was able to drink whenever he wanted, at any hour. Competent in the handling of his glass, he showed a preference for alcohol with the taste of

anise. He was a good drinker, but he was even better at gabbing and carrying on.

He was lingering all alone in the bar at sundown, nursing
his aperitif and preparing himself for the night's multiple
adventures. He didn't have to cheat in order to win at poker
in the rear parlor of the Hotel dos Lordes. He would do so
only occasionally, just to teach the contemptible cardsharps
a bit of decorum. He was astute enough to spot the nature
of the cheating and quickly figure out how to use his chips
with skill and mastery. He would unmask bluffing and put
it to use for himself with ridiculous assurance. As card play-
ers say, he could sing his opponents' tune. And he had the
gift of prophecy.

As a lover he was lavish with flattery and fancies. Going
to bed with Raduan Murad brought on disputes over the
privilege along with much cursing and cuffing among the
whores. Evil tongues whispered the names of mistresses and
married women. Virgins gazed from a distance at his slim,
impeccable figure in a white suit of H-J linen, his graying
hair, his long fingers clutching his ivory cigarette holder.
They would sigh. A bachelor well into his fifties, he was
more alluring than any young guy. Over his empty glass he
was pondering Ibrahim's fate, both a slapstick comedy and
a melodrama.

The prudent Sante, owner of the bar, had gathered in the
day's earnings, leaving just a bit of change, and he went off
to dine at home. Adib was washing glasses, mixing drinks,
putting bottles in order, and getting the bar ready for the
great nocturnal hubbub that was about to begin. Just the
right moment to pick up a conversation with the potential
candidate for the hand of Adma, at the free lunch counter.

Raduan felt an obligation to help the harassed Ibrahim in
his struggle to rise up out of his misfortune, overcome his
bad luck, and recover his right to shade and cool water, in
consideration for their old friendship, his comradeship, the
memory of Sálua's eyes, the inaccessible Sálua, but above
all, to have some fun in one more game, just as exciting as

poker—the game of destiny, already mentioned, in which the cards are human beings and the bets are for life itself.

He half-closed his eyes. Night was slowly reaching the opposite bank of the river, which was still uninhabited. Sorcery and malignancy at the crossroads for the small store. To confront the crisis, Raduan Murad's weapons were wisdom and trickery. Raising his voice, he asked Adib to give him another shot of raki, and the inquiry and negotiations got under way.

9

The exact terms of the conversation between Raduan Murad and young Adib Barud on that Itabuna twilight were never known. They carried on the dialogue alone and kept to themselves the matters discussed. But even that didn't prevent someone from reproducing the long dialogue point by point, referring to tones of voice, waves of laughter, and the depth of the silences. Some stated that the dialogue, begun in Arabic, had ended in Portuguese; others swore it was just the opposite: It had begun in Portuguese and went on in Arabic—a language, furthermore, that Adib, born as a Brazilian from southern Bahia, spoke scrupulously poorly.

To believe the generally accepted version, one still worthy of credence and repetition, when Raduan was served his drink of anise he most likely asked the waiter, "How about you? Don't you eat any dinner, young fellow?"

Adib answered yes, he did eat dinner, and quite amply. A dish prepared by Dona Lina, Sante's wife. Sante would bring it to him when he got back from home. He added a nice comment about his boss lady's looks: "Dona Lina's a knockout, don't you think, Professor? A pair of hips . . ."

In spite of the fact that Raduan wasn't a schoolmaster or even a private tutor, lots of people called him Professor, and he accepted the title without surprise or arrogance. He showed an interest in knowing just where and how Adib had been able to appraise Lina's hips. It had happened quite accidentally: Having gone to deliver a message to Sante's house, he'd found the aforementioned lady squatting and scrubbing clothes in a tub, her skirt hitched up and her hips showing. He'd chanced a peek. Besides being bold, Adib was nosy.

"There are those that say—"

Raduan, knowing full well what they were saying, cut off Adib's jabber. "Hearing always brings advantage, my boy; repeating doesn't. Forget what you've heard if you don't want to lose your job."

Lose his job? God save him and keep him! In the bar, a privileged position, Adib lived in contact with the rich and influential, the upper crust of the city, always current on happenings and stories, enjoying himself in debauchery with the whores who made their rounds there to pick up hicks. Throw away all those benefits? He'd have to be crazy.

Before that he'd toiled for three years at the Style Shop, a store belonging to his brother Aziz. Did he like it at the store? If he had to work he'd rather have the bar, for the reasons mentioned. He'd begun working behind the counter at the Style Shop for nothing, to learn the ropes. Only in the past year had he got to collect a salary, a pittance. Not being a pack mule, he'd quit.

What about as a partner? As a partner, or even just sharing in the profits, Professor, that was just a lot of talk. Because Aziz would never give him an interest in the business, no matter how much Adib killed himself with work and pleased the customers. The Style Shop of Barud and Brother? Fat chance! His ideal was to get a cacao farm— like Saad, his older brother, the son-in-law of Colonel João Cunha, who gave him a free hand, and Saad was piling up the money.

"You're not one to get involved in these things—isn't that so, Professor? You live a life that's nice and easygoing. But not everybody can live a life of comfort like a lord without working. For that you've got to have a lot of gray matter in your head."

An unexpected rascal, thought Raduan Murad, smiling good-naturedly as he listened to the unlikely commentary. How many others might there be, thinking the same thing without daring to say so? He was sorry Adib was interested in only the daughter of a plantation owner and disdainful of the daughter of a merchant. Too bad.

"Who said so, Professor? Just show me where there's one to be had and I'm off on the run after her. I've got a lot of drive behind the counter; you can ask Aziz. He's always trying to get me back, but I'd rather work for Senhor Sante. You can learn something here."

"Even if the girl's not like those beauties, maybe a little ugly?"

"No woman's ugly if she's got a little dough."

"Right you are, my boy. I can see you've had a good upbringing."

They got their good upbringing in the bosom of the home and loitering on the streets. While still adolescents they adopted and practiced the articles of the prevailing codes of the region, the unwritten but undisputed laws. When the time came to take a wife, they had to choose a virginal and virtuous woman, hardworking and upstanding, because it fell to her to give birth to and rear the children, take care of the house, and live in circumspection and modesty, be submissive. Beauty and youth are secondary qualities, especially if the principal dowry of the bride is measured in leagues of land or the number of doors on a place of business—the Bargain Shop had three doors opening onto the street. Beauty, grace, and youth are preferences when one is looking for a lover, a flirtation, or companionship for a night in bed, for a lay. In those cases, yes, the prescription calls for a pretty hooker, youngish, a fresh and cozy cunt. Healthy principles, the foundations of family and society.

"What if the one in question is a couple years older than you?" Raduan went on with his inquiry.

"What's that got to do with it, Professor? I never heard it said that age was a defect. It's just no good if she's been plowed. Covering a hole opened by someone else, that I won't do. She's got to be a virgin."

Raduan Murad paused to contemplate the young fellow, who was smiling and rubbing his hands together, excited over the direction the conversation was taking.

"If you know someone, Professor, just give me her address and I'll take care of the rest."

So why not? Adma was a rough deal, hard to swallow. Facing her called for decisiveness, courage, and the stomach of a camel. Tall, slim, muscular, doltish, Adib was like a dromedary. His youth and greed made him capable of chewing straw and finding it tasty, of standing up against an aging, sour old maid, busting her cherry with delight, raising her up into a frenzy, to beatitude, to peace with life. Well screwed, Adma would cease being a drag on humanity.

Filthy conjectures. Raduan Murad kept them to himself. He waxed poetic and wise before announcing the name of the maid in need of a husband. Certain virginities are like wine, he declared in Arabic: They improve with the passage of time and little by little they become refined, purified, and are finally transformed into liqueurs, brandy, cognac. They change their state but preserve their quality. In the heights of his curiosity and interest, Adib declared that he preferred cognac to wine.

"I know one, yes, my boy, someone who is a well of virtues, as pure as the Virgin Mary."

"Who is it, Professor? Come on. Tell me."

"Do you know Ibrahim Jafet? He was in here with me just a while ago."

"I know him, yes, sir."

"And do you know his daughters, too?"

"Them, too. Each one prettier than the next."

"Except one."

"Hold on, Professor. I'm beginning to catch the drift. You want to talk about the wallflower, right?"

"The one who marries her will become a partner in the store. . . ."

What Raduan Murad and young Adib Barud discussed and decided that late Itabuna afternoon no one knew. A lot of things were said and commented on: gossip and tales, nothing more. Sante, for example, stated that when he got back from dinner he heard Adib's final words, which, repeated to God and everyone else, became a kind of mantra.

But how could he have understood them? For Sante himself had begun by telling those listening to him that they'd been talking in Turkish. The bar owner, a flathead from Sergipe, didn't understand beans about the Arabic language, to him a complicated jawbreaker, indecipherable gabble.

In any case, inscribed here as truthful is the phrase, attributed to Adib Barud, with which the session was adjourned:

"Just leave it to me, Professor. You can tame a woman with a pat or with a whack. Or maybe with a little bit of both."

From him or from somebody else, whichever way it went, that affirmative was worthy of general acceptance and hearty approval. A surprising person, Adib Barud, the youngest son of Moamud and Ariza, both deceased. An orphan, he had educated himself haphazardly, an elegant, exquisite upbringing.

10

It could be seen immediately that Jamil Bichara and Ibrahim Jafet were twin souls, made to understand and esteem each other. The meeting took place in the cabaret. Glorinha Gold-ass introduced them. It didn't take her long to regret it. The two Turks, instead of devoting their time to her, began to gab, leaving her reduced to the ridiculous role of a deaf-mute, as though she were a piece of furniture. Wounded in her self-respect, she went off to dance with Chico Lopes, a trav-eling salesman given to the conquest of hookers. He'd been laying siege to Glorinha for some time without any success until then. The one in question didn't give of herself for free, except on those rare occasions when tricks were played on her, clouding her judgment. Not out of avarice, but from necessity. In Laranjeiras, where she had come from to ply her trade in Itabuna, she had left four sisters, devout virgins, a crippled mother, and a father who worked other people's land for his consolation of cachaça. All those and, in ad-dition, two loony aunts—"my dearly beloved creatures," she would weep with longing as she remembered them—all dependent on her, on the little money she would send each month by Aureliano Neves, the owner of the Casa Ser-gipana, first-class furniture, her parishioner on Saturdays.

The youngest daughter, a flirtatious mulatto girl in full bloom, had given her cherry for free to the judge's son, that son of a bitch, who after making a great fuss over her had kicked her out as soon as she'd been fucked, to the fury of her drunken but moralistic father, without even a good-bye. He'd promised to set her up in a house, all established, for a

love affair. In some strange way she was grateful to him
because when he'd popped her cherry he'd brought her good
luck. The divine Glorinha went off to be a whore in cacao
country, Glorinha Goldass, sought after. The fulsome pledges
of the traveling salesman went in one ear and out the
other, in spite of his elegant mustache and his hair that
gleamed with brilliantine and was parted down the middle
just like a pussy, the height of fashion. The dandy danced
well, and Glorinha wasn't far behind him in that. She
adored waltzes, polkas, mazurkas, but the best of all was
the maxixe.

Interest on Jamil's part was there right from the start
when, rejoicing in the unexpected appearance of the ideal
candidate, Ibrahim went straight to the business at hand.
On that afternoon the person of his fellow countryman was
still the center of attention, the object of conversation and
speculation. Raduan Murad, a friend in common, a man of
great aptitude, had proposed the name of Jamil, and he had
regretted his absence. What had his name been proposed
for? To solve a problem of interest for Ibrahim, but one that
might be of equal interest for Jamil. He would like to lay it
out if his countryman would care to listen and set a time
and place. Right here and now was his answer. He didn't
have any time the following day, completely taken up with
replenishing his stock and shipping out the merchandise.
The mixture of vermouth and cognac had loosened the
tongue of Adma's afflicted father. All ears, out of natural
prudence Jamil wasn't showing any enthusiasm for the scheme
at any time.

Before even getting into the details of the tangled hodge-
podge, Jamil declared he was quite satisfied with the place
where he lived and did business. He had no intention of leaving it. He hadn't grown wealthy yet, no, but if houses kept on
being built his store for mule drivers would become an important business just as sure as two and two make four. Do you
know Colonel Noberto de Faria? Just ask him and he'll tell
you so. If he let go of something that had cost him so much
privation, effort, and sacrifice and that promised a wealthy

future, it would have to be for an offer of something that was really worthwhile.

At the start of the negotiations, Ibrahim offered him the position of manager, with a salary and a small share of the profits. He watered the proposal with some vermouth. Jamil laughed to his face with that great whiplike guffaw he used when he set prices for small farmers, hired hands, and gunmen in that cacao-growing last end of the earth. At that moment in the wrangle Glorinha Goldass got them even angrier as she went on praising Chico Lopes, a perfect gentleman—and he had such a nice way with words! The opposite of the two rude and ignorant Turks, who'd left her there all by herself. What in hell had Jamil come to the cabaret for in the first place? To have a good time, to get his thoughts far away from what was bugging him? Or was it to spend the night in that endless gabbing with Ibrahim? Ibrahim, another numbskull, instead of taking up all her man's time, should have been looking for a woman to sleep with himself before the colonels grabbed all those present, leaving him without a howdy-do. She was right. Jamil gave her his arm and led her to the dance floor. Ibrahim took advantage of the break and the advice as he spotted Cockeye Paula all by herself beside the orchestra. He invited her for a polka. But both of them, Jamil and Ibrahim, were dancing without any interest in it, paying no attention, their minds set on their machinations.

When they got back to the table Ibrahim put forth the possibility of a partnership if Adma were included in the transaction. In that way the other daughters and their re- spective husbands would have no grounds for complaint. Other daughters, which ones? What tune were those new sons-in-law playing? While Glorinha was taking care of her invitations from plantation owners and traveling salesmen for square dances and rejecting offers to leave the cabaret and the Turk—Colonel Raimundo Barreto threatened to carry her off by force, but she, with great skill, convinced him to take somebody else—the two fellow countrymen, between successive rounds of vermouth and cognac, were advancing, detail by detail, trying to untangle the thread. Ibrahim, although drunk, controlled himself and didn't vomit up the final secrets. He made it honorably clear that his daughter Adma didn't figure in the gallery of local beauties. About her character he revealed nothing. There's time for everything even when you're in a hurry.

"If I understand it right, my friend, you want to retire— you've already worked too much; you feel tired. You want someone you can trust who's able to take your place behind the counter in the store, since your son-in-law can't cut it. On the other hand, you've got an unmarried daughter and you want to set her up. Putting the two ends together, whoever marries the girl becomes a partner in the busines. . . ."

They left the cabaret early in the morning. Ibrahim, a lightweight when it came to drinking, was staggering along the street. Cockeye Paula hadn't kept her promise to wait for him and had gone off with a bad-tempered plantation owner, a certain Cláudio Portugal, crazy for cross-eyed girls.

"Promise me and don't give me any shit! Either you come with me, or I'll save some time and finish off those bums right now. . . ." He threatened to pull out his pistol.

The owner of the Bargain Shop consoled himself with stuffy-nosed Haydée, who made up for the nasality of her voice with a range of skills. In the state capital she'd worked in a house of French and Polish women, and she could do anything, according to her whim.

In Glorinha Goldass's room the lamp cast its light on the mirror hanging on the wall and the print of Saint George. The sheets and pillowcases smelled of patchouli. While he waited for the angry woman to clean herself over a basin in preparation for resuming their game of bird and snare, Jamil reviewed the facts he'd collected. Before he went any further, he would have to bring out into the open the true condition of the store, the confused business of the partnership, observe the daughters and sons-in-law, and lastly, get to know the ugly one. He had been destined to have a pretty wife, but in the backwoods wilderness where he did his business, in that out-of-the-way place where he'd set himself up, small farmers were used to eating well one day and poorly the next, on vermin and weeds, without complaining or raising a fuss. In the harsh weather of the cacao farms, mules, mares, and donkeys all grazed and came out okay.

11

Even though he was tied up all the next day with suppliers, goods, and payments, Jamil Bichara found time to have a look at the store. From the brief inventory done with the help of Ibrahim, he came away with a favorable impression, which he kept to himself. He wasn't going to trumpet his triumphs to his adversary. He called attention to the negative aspects: the delay in payments, the decline in sales, negligence, incompetence.

The lively Alfeu and the merry cherub felt they were on an eternal honeymoon, a romantic and ruinous attitude. Nighttime was not sufficient for their screwing, which they continued well into the morning. Added to that was the baby's wailing, the changing of diapers, pacifiers. It was impossible to keep a tight schedule. They opened and closed the doors of the establishment when it suited their fancy. Drowsy, they continued their billing and cooing behind the counter without giving proper attention to the seamstresses and housewives who, in exchange for a few small purchases—a thimble, a dozen buttons, hairpins, two yards of ribbon—demanded a little talk and consideration.

Sálua's clientele, which had been faithful and numerous, had begun to dwindle, leaving for merchants less in love and more solicitous. Nor was the proprietor much help to the store's progress. The night before in the cabaret, Ibrahim had confessed he had been completely detached from the store during his wife's life. Sálua had taken care of all obligations and responsibilities and also kept the accounts. He remembered Sálua with moist eyes. Were these easy tears a touch of cunning, or the expression of a sincere and sorrowful longing for a good life and a good home?

In spite of its obvious decline, the Bargain Shop, located on a downtown street, a privileged site with plenty of room, looked to Jamil like a gift from China. The recent difficulties had shaken up only slightly the good reputation the firm had enjoyed in the business world during all those previous years. In capable hands the store would be able to recoup its golden years quite quickly, and it had the makings of being transformed, with a little effort, into a well-stocked bazaar where a little of everything would be sold: men's and women's clothing, shoes and hats, suspenders, bows, stockings, and neckties. All that called for a strong hand, an aptitude for business, and hard work, proven virtues of Jamil Bichara. The problem lay in the number of daughters and sons-in-law, too many people. If he decided to join the family and the firm, he would have to make a serious study of the clauses in the contract.

They were going over bills and receipts when, from the living quarters in the rear and into the store, came a slender little tootsie, who kissed Jamil's countryman's hand—"Your blessing, Father"—and smiled at Jamil as her curious and calculating eyes examined him from top to bottom, as though evaluating his merits as a male. Could she be the ugly one? Impossible. There was nothing ugly about her; quite the contrary.

"My daughter Samira," Ibrahim explained. "The one who's married to the telegrapher."

"Jamil Bichara, at your service."

"Jamil Bichara? I've heard that name before. . . ."

"He's a friend of my old chum Raduan."

"Of Uncle Raduan? Oh, now I remember." She pointed at Jamil and said mischievously, "The sultan of the cabaret, right?"

Jamil laughed, a bit embarrassed. "Sultan's what he calls me. He has his little joke. . . ."

The lively girl kept looking him over, and all of a sudden she burst into a peal of crystalline and mocking laughter, without explaining what had brought it on. Uncle Raduan had bits of gossip for the interest and pleasure of anyone who wished to listen, but he kept his spicy tales of bohemian life for Samira and a few other preferred women, revealing places and episodes forbidden to married ladies. Uncle Raduan was the Devil incarnate, with that velvety voice and the most innocent of looks as he divulged every little tidbit. In order to explain his friend Jamil's success with the hookers, he'd make reference to one aspect of his anatomy: It was enormous, like a table leg. Judging from his great build, it must have been true. Samira closed her eyes to give herself a better picture.

As for Uncle Raduan, since he wasn't a blood relative, there was nothing to stop his gossiping to bring on laughs and pass the time. The double entendres, the hints, the spicy tone, the inconsequential flirting were all fine. Necking and nooky, those were the pleasures of Samira, who had been destined for a storybook marriage. Exchanging glances and smiles, dubious words, feeling the surreptitious touch of a foot, a hand, a lip, by chance or by intent, could anything be better? There were those who called her shameless and said she had put horns on Esmeraldino the riddle maker; others swore that Samira wouldn't go that far with her liberties. She'd play along, all right, but at H-hour she'd drop out, the little cheat, with her I-never-said-that.

As she bent over to pick up a spool of thread in front of Jamil, she let him take in the curve of her loose breasts. Wanting to or not, who can tell? Before leaving she ran the tip of her tongue over her lips, as if they were dry. Dry or thirsty, whichever way you want to interpret it. A sister-in-law isn't a relative, Jamil reflected. Going over the accounts again in his mind, he placed Samira in the column of the store's assets.

course of the evening Jamil had proof of the Lord's indifference. He hadn't bestowed one single shitty bit of it.

Jamil was given a knockout punch when he faced Adma upon their introduction. But being who he was, one hardened by ambushes, by the quid pro quos of life, he didn't immediately drop right then and there his idea of transforming the Bargain Shop into the bazaar with the most goods and the most customers in Itabuna. He'd thought of finding an ugly old maid on whose uninviting face was reflected, however, enough natural goodness that almost reached the point of rendering her pretty. Ugly but pleasant, active at household chores, genteel in manner, a charming conversationalist, all in all an affable old maid whose only defect consisted in not being pretty. Thinking that, he came face-to-face with a hag, a toad-faced hag!

Sitting across from Jamil, Adma was governing the table from one end to the other, reproving with her look, her gestures, and her voice anything that might have meant merriment, laughter, and contentment. She was harsh in her condemnation of a new very funny riddle put forth by Esmeraldino to test the guests' intelligence.

"Listen! Listen! It's quite easy. What everyday action can turn you into someone filthy?"

He looked around triumphantly and then gave the answer himself. "Walking down the street. That makes you a streetwalker, a prostitute. Ha ha ha!"

Very good, very good, a nice riddle. The cherub clapped her hands, all worked up by her brother-in-law's ingenious invention. "Indecent!" thundered Adma. Indecent were the kisses exchanged by Alfeu and Fárida between mouthfuls; intolerable was the satisfied belching of Ibrahim, his belly full. She didn't dare interrupt Raduan Murad, but she tightened her face as she listened to him declaiming poetry in Arabic about women and wine: filth! Immune to the noisy jollity, apart from the general well-being, intolerant and unhappy. At a certain moment, in order to serve the coffee better, Samira leaned over in front of Jamil, and her neighbor had no way of preventing his eyes from landing on the

12

Had it not been for the presence of Adma, the dinner would have been perfect. A most tasty Arab meal prepared by Samira with the help of Fárida the cherub, who had also picked some flowers to decorate the table, as if the two of them were not enough, exotic, dressed and coiffed in the latest style. They were sorry about the absence of Jamile, hidden away on the farm along with her husband. Speaking of husbands, Samira's, the telegrapher, was in attendance and scintillating, cordial and good-natured, showing a gluttonous appreciation of the kibbe and the esfiha. Making for a refined sense of well-being were Raduan Murad, wise and witty, and Samira's right knee, as she was seated to the left of Jamil. She didn't know how to sit still.

Unfortunately there was also Adma, a baleful figure but an indispensable guest. In order for Jamil to get a look at her and chat with her, Ibrahim had invited him to dine with the family in their upstairs living quarters. Cautious, he'd said nothing to his daughters about the plan he was hatching. To do so before his countryman had met the intended would have been foolhardy.

No sooner did Jamil set eyes upon Adma than he realized the enormous challenge. It wasn't any use to bedeck her in bows and ribbons, cute trinkets from the store. It was insufficient compensation for her complete lack of physical attributes. Adma would have to be a saint on an altar for any citizen in possession of his faculties to decide to take her in matrimony. May God bestow that sainthood! During the open neck of her dress. That was enough for Adma to lock her sister in a deadly stare, along with the hateful guest and the heedless riddler. Jamil trembled.

The malignant look of accusation and repugnance followed Jamil outside when, after dinner, gathering up his courage, Ibrahim asked the gentlemen present. "Shall we take a walk around the square, to help digest our food?"

With the exception of Alfeu, still on his honeymoon, as has been noted, and Esmeraldino, who started along but held back when Samira wanted to know, "So who's going to take me home?" addressing her husband without taking her roguish eyes off Jamil.

The others picked up their hats and headed for the whorehouse. Raduan Murad wondered if there was still any salvation for poor Adma. Maybe it was too late and neither young Adib, with his adolescent gawkiness, or the gigantic Jamil, with his immense tool, could rescue her from her madness, from the fires of hell, save her from the curse of her hardened virginity and teach her, in bed, the love of life.

13

Ibrahim stopped midsentence. He tried to get up from his chair and slipped down under the table, from where they pulled him up with the help of the waiters. The meeting was adjourned, and Jamil resolved to take his countryman to the door of his house. He would never get there by himself. His legs wouldn't hold him up.

Sad and weepy, Ibrahim had spent most of the night thinking about the dead woman. All that love was very moving for the whores who had gathered around the table to listen to him. Some of them had known Sálua when she was behind the counter at the Bargain Shop, where they went to shop for adornments for their dresses, fine combs, fancy rings. A married and rich lady owner—and such a beauty!—Sálua had made no distinctions among her customers, treating all of them with the same courtesy, whether mothers with a family or licentious harlots.

Sharing Ibrahim's feelings, they remembered that during his wife's lifetime he was a model husband—a terrible example for the community in the majority opinion of the heads of families. He never frequented the cabaret, nor did he spend the night in bawdy houses, and if he did happen to do so, it was with an idea to forget it, but he never forgot. On the occasion of a festive dinner at home, so frequent when she was alive, so rare after her death, the weight of her absence became unbearable. Cockeye Paula, the sentimental reader of serialized novels that came out every Thursday, would burst into tears. A love like the one that joined Sálua and Ibrahim could be found only in the one between Paul and Virginie, and even then!

Jamil had come to realize that the widower had very little or no wisdom at all, never going beyond being just a nice fellow. He would listen to his laments with silent sympathy as he got ready to take him home. Raduan Murad had left sometime earlier, off to his duties at the poker table, but Jamil could count on the help of Glorinha Goldass and Cockeye Paula. Among the three of them they led Ibrahim and his cross in fits and starts up to the vicinity of his store.

At the sound of footsteps, a shutter on the second floor opened. A storm of insults broke the silence of the night. Posted at the window, Adma, the mouth of hell, was spewing out imprecations, accusations, complaints, and threats at her father, the Cyrenaic, and the Magdalens. It was really something to behold. Raduan Murad had witnessed such a spectacle only once, and he'd had to have recourse to unusual terms to classify it: Catilinarian, vespine, atrabilious.

The two whores fell back, and Ibrahim sobbed on Jamil's shoulder. Adma went on, an insatiable fury, waking up the whole neighborhood. Ibrahim made an effort to get his balance and headed off to the gates of Calvary. Before he crossed the threshold he lifted his arms and waved them about in the gesture of a drowning man. Adma was unmoved, nor did she relent. Pointing to Jamil, she thundered her last words.

Quickening his pace, the Turk caught up with his companions in fun, who were fleeing down the street. Cockeye Paula, offended, remarked, "Goddamned daughter! Ibrahim's a softy. If he took the whip to that willful bitch, her rotten mood would stop right there."

With her usual gentility, Glorinha Goldass offered a better alternative. "What she needs, poor thing, is a good dick."

As he thought about it, Jamil found them both to be right. Suffering from a grave illness, a hopeless one, Adma, if she was to be cured, stood in urgent need of both remedies, the dick and the whip, in generous doses. In which, without knowing it, he was in agreement with young Adib: You tame a woman with pats and slaps.

14

For two months, an eternity, the Turk Jamil Bichara lived
the problem at its fullest, pondering it down to its smallest
details, analyzing it from all kinds of angles. At the station
where he was taking the train to Mutuns, he said to Ibrahim,
"I need time to think before I make any decision. When I get
back I'll have an answer for you. In the meantime, look after
the store a little and take charge at home."

In the wilds of Itaguassu, with Shaitan tempting Jamil
ceaselessly night and day, Ibrahim's proposal was looking
better, ever more attractive and enticing. Allah seemed to be
staying on the sidelines, indifferent. He'd abandoned Jamil
at that decisive moment, leaving the responsibility entirely in
his hands.

Seen from the miserable hamlet where he was hard at
work, the city of Itabuna—lively and turbulent, with its
businesses, church, and chapel, the Lords Hotel, cabaret,
bars, houses with ladies of the night, its cobblestone streets,
the hustle and bustle at the station with the daily arrival
and departure of the passenger train, the intrigues of politics
and landgrabs, the hired guns, the mule trains unloading
cacao at the great warehouses of the export companies—
was becoming a regular capital city. In Itabuna you lived; in
Itaguassu you suffered.

Glorinha Goldass would work him up, as usual, disturb-
ing his sleep, offering herself to him naked, lewd, and inaccessible. She would be joined by another demanding lure, a
more delicate temptation, a married lady, Samira Jafet Esmeraldino. Her saucy knee, her loose, abundant breasts, just

right for grabbing and squeezing with your hands, her crafty
look, a look that was on the make, her wet tongue over dry
lips, Samira whispering, "Come here, come here right now,
I'm waiting for you, a sister-in-law isn't a blood relative, no."
Which of the two was the more desirable, the trickier? Two
mistakes were leading him astray: the whore in a cathouse
and the other one even more.

Most of all, however, weighing on the balance was the
prospect of reviving the store in just a short time and immediately turning it into a bazaar, well furnished with merchandise, provided with everything fine and good, a business
with lots of customers, fat profits. Once he was declared
chief of the clan, Jamil would lay down the law benevo-
lently. He imagined himself behind the counter, aided by his
sisters-in-law Samira and Fárida. Instead of staying home
sucking on a lollipop or in boobish conversation with people
at the station, Samira, young and robust, would be of obvious help in the store, making her pleasant manner useful. By
the same token, Fárida would be a beautiful presence, pleas-
ing to the customers' eyes, and the masculine clientele would
increase just as soon as the Bargain Shop was changed into
a bazaar. As for the agreeable Alfeu, back at his true vocation at the English Haberdashery, there he could fulfill his
enviable career, advancing from apprentice to journeyman,
from journeyman to master tailor, ceasing to represent any
threat to the store's finances.

It's worth repeating what everybody knows quite well: A
sister-in-law is not a blood relative, but family ties do permit
an intimacy that could be called fraternal. Jamil's horizons
were expanding: a sultan with his harem. That, yes, was
living.

Jamil studied minutely the clauses in the contract to be
drawn up at the notary's office. Partnership on Adma's side
from her mother's inheritance, partner with Ibrahim on his
side in his role as manager of the business. Given over to his
leisure activities, Ibrahim would stay on as a kind of silent
partner, with Jamil in the position of complete authority
with the right to do and undo things.

He foresaw buying out the shares of Jamile and of Ranulfo, her husband, at the start. Anyone who owns a cacao farm has no other ambition in life beyond acquiring land and more land for planting, increasing his holdings and his harvests. He's not interested in stores and businesses. Later on Jamil would study what actions could be taken with regard to the shares owned by his other sisters-in-law. It would depend on their good behavior and that of their husbands. In his idle hours the emoluments of the project kept increasing and taking over his thoughts.

Even the very ugliness of Adma, an aggressive harridan, a slab of dry cod, faded off into the distance. Shaitan the trickster couldn't hide that reality, nor did he have the powers to do that much. But he did manage to suppress or blur the details, reducing her little mustache to just thick fuzz and transforming her sour, tight mouth into a sign of dignity. After all, Jamil had knocked off others more hideous and repulsive without getting sick, paying in coin of the realm and running the risk of catching some venereal disease, syph or the clap.

Besides, it must be kept in mind that certain ugly women are irresistible. They've got their own mysteries, as Raduan Murad had once said, when Jamil commented with amazement at the extravagance of Salim Hadad, a millionaire fellow countryman, a plantation owner with his twenty thousand tons between ripening and harvest. Married to a cousin, Yasmina, a fine chunk of a woman, a real dish, he was all caught up with the lowest slut on the Rua do Umbuzeiro, Silvinha, a snotty face, a filthy ass, the breasts of a hag, a streetwalker. He spent a fortune on her. How do you explain something as absurd as that?

"She had her mysteries, Jamil. A creature can look ugly, be in the worst shape, but if her lower mouth is worth a kiss, it's like a pure diamond, something incomparable. Between you and me, I guarantee it. I know no equal to Silvinha's downstairs mouth. . . ." He clicked his tongue in nostalgic affirmation.

Who knows, maybe Adma is one of those privileged

creatures, a divine pussy, worth a sucking. Jamil didn't really believe it, but it wasn't impossible either. Right there in Itaguassu was the example of Laurinha, nicknamed the Witch. A witch to scare the hell out of you. With the lamp out, in the dark, and with your thoughts on something else, there was no one who could compare with her, a twidget as tight as a virgin girl's, a body's mouth that quivered when it was tippled.

It was more difficult to soften the rough spots of Adma's character. Jamil couldn't forget the malignant presence of the shrew at dinner, even less Ibrahim's martyrdom. He could see himself coming home from the cabaret in the middle of the night or from Afonsina's house early in the morning. A husband shouldn't have any set time for arriving home or have to give an accounting. He'd find Adma up in the window waiting for him, in a foul mood, waking up the neighbors as she repeated her scoldings, a wild uproar. If she tried to get on his back the way she did with Ibrahim, would a dick and a whip be enough? He doubted it.

Abandoned by Allah to the seductions of Shaitan, left to his own devices, he spent two months in that battle with nothing decided. But at every moment the Evil One would strengthen his hold over Jamil's soul. Before heading out to Mutuns, where he got the train to Itabuna, Jamil considered Ibrahim's proposal impossible to refuse: a well-established business, a fortune in sight, and a woman with excellent qualities. He was thinking of Samira, not Adma.

For Adma, not much dick and lots of whip. Unless the hag was in possession (she had her mysteries, too) of an incomparable twat, one made for sucking. "It's quite possible; it's almost certain," the Devil was whispering behind him.

15

Could Allah and his prophet Mohammed be so little concerned with the destiny of their son Jamil Bichara that they would forget the pact of faith and assistance that existed between them and not even draw his attention to the dangers of the enterprise he was insisting on getting involved in? More likely they had attempted to do so, and the obstinate fellow had refused to lend them an ear. "I was blind and deaf," Jamil himself confessed to Raduan Murad. "I surrendered to the temptation of gold and of the flesh. Shaitan was living in my heart."

According to the adage, God writes clearly with crooked lines, and in order to bring his designs to completion, he makes use of strange methods, moves unexpected characters about. While Shaitan, encamped in Itaguassu, was dedicating all his time to the seduction of Jamil, Allah the great was maneuvering in Itabuna to save his soul and to defend the future of his anointed one.

As things turned out, as he reviewed with Jamil the developments in the skirmish, Raduan, who'd followed it detail by detail, eagerly when he became aware of Shaitan's involvement—lewd dreams, foul enticements, exaggerated and dubious promises—found Allah's strategy and tactics to be superior in all ways. Not only from having put the enemy face-to-face with a consummated fact, but also from the way in which he'd done it: Instead of any subjective study or thundering actions worthy of the best traditions of the Old Testament, he'd brought it forth in full form. He began a most beautiful performance with the romantic and heroic episode of the stampeding herd, the first in a series of magnificent and spectacular ploys.

The string of donkeys stampeded for no apparent reason just before reaching the warehouses of Kuntz & Co., a Swiss cacao exporting firm. The animals shot off in a headlong run, befouling, befarting, and knocking down pedestrians during a time of intense activity. Sacks fell from the wooden frames of the packsaddles, cacao beans scattered into the gutters, people were fleeing madly; it was the end of the world.

At that exact moment the maiden Adma had just stepped out onto the tumultuous thoroughfare, returning from Samira's house on the Largo da Estação, where she'd been making her sister's life hell. She'd even talked about Jamil Bichara, calling him names, while Samira came to his defense and that of their father: One a bachelor, the other a widower, they had every right to visit whorehouses. The mood grew sour and Adma was close to having a fainting spell when the desirable one accused her of being intolerant because she hadn't found anyone who wanted her. Nothing could have wounded her more deeply.

She was coming along the middle of the street, head down and unhappy, when she heard the shouting and the braying and saw before her the shapes of the maddened beasts, under whose hooves she was going to die, crushed. In spite of everything, Adma had no wish to die. She didn't have the strength to flee, so she let out a wail, closed her eyes, and waited for the blow, the fall, the shoes on the hooves, the end. In a faint, she felt herself being snatched up into the air.

When she opened her eyes she could see that eternal life had begun and she had deserved paradise: Before her was an archangel, bending over her and smiling, celestial, dazzling. It wasn't paradise; it was the inside of a dry-goods store. Someone was holding a glass to her mouth as the water ran down from the corners of her lips. The echoes of the tumult and the shouts of the donkey drivers could still be heard. The archangel wasn't wearing wings, but he kept on staring at her. A fat man, all covered with sweat and fright, all flustered, was explaining things.

"A narrow escape. You had a narrow escape. You were born again. This young fellow here risked his life; he's a hero." He was pointing to the archangel, with the admiration of the people crowding at the door to get a better look.

Adma looked up at the hero. He'd lost his celestial origins, but he was still young and strong, and he kept on smiling. She still found him dazzling. He politely gave her his hand to help her up from the chair where they'd seated her and said, "Let's go, Adma! I'm going to take you home."

Adma felt weak and confused, not understanding immediately what was going on. She was still under the shock of it all. Where did the prince know her from? How had he learned her name? Confused, she accepted the hand he was holding out to her, but she was unsteady on her feet as she stood up, so he held her, taking her arm.

"Lean on my arm. Let's go, sweetie."

Sweetie, a most loving name, a most courteous one.

16

For the first time in her life Adma found herself walking down the street arm in arm with a man. The man in question had called her sweetie and was smiling at her with a smile full of implications.

"Don't you remember me?"

She would have liked to answer yes, that she did remember, how could she have forgotten. Unhappily, alas, she couldn't remember when she'd seen him. Never in her life, fatter or skinnier, it was amazing, never. Perplexed, she smiled as he refreshed her memory.

"I used to work at the Style Shop, which belongs to my brother Aziz. Don't you remember? I'd be there spying on you, wanting you. . . ."

He'd been spying, wanting? She had never been aware of it.

A warmth came into her skinny breast. She hadn't realized it, but there were men who spied on her, young men, fascinating princes, angels from heaven who wanted her. The most marvelous thing happened when they got near the house.

"I used to pass by here every day just to see you in the window, but you never noticed me."

Adma stopped walking, wanting to hear him repeat that he'd passed by there. Just to see her? Alas, she couldn't believe it! She would have given anything for Samira to be there now, seeing and listening, dying with envy. With difficulty she explained, "We have to go in by the street in back. I went out through the gate in the yard."

They turned away, the key trembling in Adma's hand.
The prince, still smiling, took it and opened the ancient lovers' portal. The old maid entered, eyes down. She didn't
have the courage to look at the one who had saved her from
death, who had taken her arm and told her what she had
never heard before. It could be only a vision, on the point of
vanishing.

"I don't know how to thank you; you saved my life!"

She was speaking in the yard, in a low voice. It was the
end of the enchantment. There he was, going off forever.
The road to happiness had been short. She'd been able
to get only a glimpse of paradise. She was returning to hell
again.

"You don't know, good-looking?" Adib Barud, the archangel, the hero, the prince, the hickish dromedary, smiled
wider, with openly good or bad intentions now, according
to how one sees it. He winked and announced, "Well, then,
I'm going to show you right now, my beauty." He repeated, "My beauty" and added, ready for anything, "My little
knockout!"

He went through the gate and gave it a shove, closing it.
With one of his hands he grabbed Adma around the waist;
with the other he held her head as her knot of hair came
undone. She lost her voice and her movement. Adib held her
in a kiss he'd learned from Procópia, the civil judge's woman.
A storm of kisses, tongues, and teeth, marking her mouth
and her soul forever. She struggled, but he held her tight.
Adma's body finally softened as she fainted into Adib's arms.
It had been too much for one day. He supported her against
the wall and leaned on her. He ran his hand up and down, a
pleasant surprise. The ironing board had breasts, and they
weren't limp or fallen.

Neither limp nor fallen, just one more grace of God on
that afternoon of miracles. No one had fallen under the
hooves of the animals; the cacao had been picked up grain
by grain. There was no damage worth complaining about.
As for Adib's presence at the scene of the drama, it wasn't
because of any supernatural coincidence. Ever since his chat

with Raduan Murad, the boy from the bar had been looking for the right opportunity to speak to Adma about matters of love. When he saw her pass on her way back from the station, he asked Sante's permission to leave and followed her closely. The rest fell to God to do, and he did it with magnificence, skill, and speed, as everyone can attest.

17

"Today the drinks are on me," announced Ibrahim Jafet after ordering a round of anisette.

He took over the chair left by the druggist Napoleão Sabóia, the only native champion capable of standing up to the invincible Syrio-Lebanese at the backgammon board.

Lowering his voice, he whispered in Raduan Murad's ear, "Yesterday I celebrated two weeks, old friend."

"Two weeks, Ibrahim? A whole two weeks?"

Yes, two whole weeks had passed without the old maid Adma's waiting with curses and insults for her father's arrival in the predawn hours, without the usual uproar. Some of the neighbors sensed that something was missing. Something inexplicable was happening. Adma didn't seem to be herself at all. Ibrahim was even capable of swearing that he'd seen her smile more than once in the past few days. Two weeks of complete tranquility, no witchcraft to disturb him in the critical moment of shooting his load, preventing him from exercising his status as a male with ardor and competence—he'd stopped going limp.

"What can you tell me, old friend? What explanation can you give me?"

Raduan couldn't find any immediate explanation, but he went on to conceive and accumulate suspicions in proportion to the growth of unexpected actions on the part of young Adib, always hanging about his table. For no rhyme or reason, when their eyes crossed, the waiter would smile or wink, smiles and winks of complicity. On a certain occasion he whispered in his ear, rubbing his hands,"Everything's

going fine, Professor!" The suspicions were ripening in the
direction of what Adib might have to do with the mysteri-
ous transformation of Adma.

Weeks went by with no great incidents except for the
shooting at the Caga-Fumo, in which two women and three
men died, an ordinary fight between gunmen in a whorehouse; and the murder of Dr. Felício de Carvalho, the law-
yer for parties opposed to Colonel Amílcar Teles in the
Pedra Branca deal, a settling of old accounts. A mediocre balance for a period of a month and a half—could it have been
that the bustle of Itabuna was going into decline? Well,
on one of those late backgammon afternoons, when Raduan Murad was left all alone in the bar, sipping his last
glass of the bogus anisette, counterfeited by the Mohana
family and delicious, better than the imported variety, Adib
came over to him.

"May I, Professor? Do you remember that talk we had
the other day?"

"Talk? Which one?" Raduan was playing innocent.

"About marriage, et cetera and so forth. You told me,
Professor . . ."

"Now I remember."

"I'm an orphan on both sides, you know. I'd like you,
Professor, to have a talk with Mr. Ibrahim as if you were
my father. I want to marry his daughter."

"You want to marry Adma?" He held back an expression
of surprise. Astonished, he remained silent for a moment
and looked straight at Adib with obvious wonderment.

"What about Adma? Does she know about your intentions?"

"We've been making love going on two months now."

"Making love? How? She up in the window and you
down in the street? Sending little billets-doux?"

"Little notes, Professor? Not with me! It's right in the
backyard. When I leave here at ten o'clock at night, she's
waiting for me. She leaves the gate open." He clicked his
tongue in an obscene sound of satisfaction, identical to the

one he gave months before when he recalled Procópia, the civil judge's woman.

"You mean . . . ?"

"Just what you're thinking, Professor. You know what it's like. People start fooling around, a touch here, a pat there; then when you realize it, it's too late—the meeting's already been called to order."

An amazing individual! Trying to clarify things for him, perhaps, he only ended up leaving Raduan in the dark, all confused, as he swore he was.

"Maybe you can't imagine it, Professor, but she's really something." He smiled with contentment and satisfaction. Raduan Murad was fascinated.

"Tell Mr. Ibrahim he can put the store in my hands. In my hands it's going to be a first-class bazaar."

From whom had Raduan heard an affirmative just like that?

"I'll see to the matter," he said, accepting the assignment. Conceding it its deserved importance, he added: "This request calls for a celebration, speeches. It's not every day that an engagement like this comes along, one so . . ." He searched for the adjective. "Auspicious."

He sat there thinking for a moment and then turned to Adib. "Really something! Is that what you said, Adib my boy?"

"Really something!" the young man confirmed.

Raduan Murad preserved in his memory the expression he hadn't been familiar with. Absorbed in it all, he turned his eyes toward the sky, which was breaking into fire over the outlying parts of Itabuna.

18

As he passed by the doors of the Bargain Shop, Jamil Bichara grew indignant at the sight of bars on the doors that early in the evening, when there was a lot of commercial activity. It was absurd, something that called for urgent measures and quick action. He'd try to see to that and put an end to the mess.

He went over to the entrance to the family quarters and began to climb the stairs. He could hear the sound of voices coming from the living room. At the top he found the door wide open. He peeked inside before clapping his hands and asking permission to enter. From what he could see, a solemn ceremony was taking place, in the presence of a lot of people. Who knows, maybe it was a mournful but animated wake. Had there been a death in the family? Maybe the persecuted Ibrahim had committed suicide, unable to bear any longer the crisis that had overcome the business and the family. Only something like that could explain the closing of the store and the somber Sunday clothes of the unknown couple standing on the threshold of the foyer. He recognized Raduan Murad, who was making a speech in Arabic, probably the funeral eulogy for his friend. He was filled with sadness and remorse, but he immediately discarded the funeral theory when he heard the crystalline and licentious laughter of Samira, one of the principal reasons for his being there to say yes.

But the one who was saying yes was the master of the house, the head of the clan, Ibrahim Jafet, brimming with good health and satisfaction, euphoric. He was giving his agreement as father to the request of Raduan Murad, who had just made it with an inspired toast. He was giving the hand of his daughter Adma to Adib Barud, who from that day forward would also be his son.

Jamil appeared in the room just at the moment of toasting by the members of the Jafet and Barud families, gathered in celebration, one that was all the more sensational for being unexpected. He was introduced to Jamile, his other almost sister-in-law, her husband, Ranulfo Pereira, and Adib's brothers and sisters-in-law. He knew Adib from the bar, but he never would have imagined him involved with Adma. The damnedest things!

He was able to contemplate with fine impartiality the ominous maiden, and he couldn't know how he had come to accept—even desire!—marriage with her. Seeing her so submissive on the arm of her fiancé, dripping with giggles and coquetry, was repugnant to him. He concluded that not even in exchange for the kingdom of the Thousand and One Nights would a normal citizen subject himself to such an infamous pact. That young fellow Adib Barud, besides being a base, greedy boy, was a degenerate. And yet, less than an hour before, Jamil was climbing the stairs to the living quarters with the aim of putting forth, in plain language, a request identical to the one Raduan Murad had transmitted with poetical emotion in the name of the ex-waiter. Greed just as base. A degenerate? Oh, no! Possessed by Shaitan, bewitched, blind, and deaf.

He raised his glass to drink a toast along with Sante to the health of the betrothed. The bar owner, accompanied by his wife, Lina, the one with the attractive hips, was lamenting the loss of his valuable employee, a hard worker, discreet in his thievery. He foresaw a brilliant future for him in the new business. The drinks were good and they were free, the company pleasant. Jamil Bichara took part in the general merriment. An unexpected guest, he was one of the most expansive.

Talking foolishness with Samira by a window ledge, this

time it fell to Jamil to break out suddenly in uncontrollable laughter.

"What are you laughing at so heartily?" the flirtatious girl wanted to know.

"I'm laughing at Shaitan," Jamil Bichara answered, and it was the truth.

19

Jamil Bichara got out of the mess unharmed, with no great damage. The profits he had imagined back in the wilds of Itaguassu, the fortune, the sultanate, were nothing but daydreams. They would have been hard to bring off. They might easily have vanished into nothing, leaving him with obligations and the marriage on his back. The marriage: Hoo-whee! Holy shit!

He conserved his friendship with Ibrahim, a jovial companion for nights of carousing, and he continued his inconsequential flirtations with Samira. He would go visit her on the Largo da Estação every time he came to Itabuna. They would chat about foolish things, exchange smiles, hints, vague promises, tender squeezing of hands. There would be casual touching here and there, peeking into the neck of her dress, but it never went beyond that. He'd have his rewards in his dreams in Itaguassu, where Samira would relax with him on nights of debauchery—full breasts, broad belly, bushy little precipice. Allah had saved him from Adma and a horrible fate as a pack mule, killing himself in work to sustain the lazybones Jafet family. As a small compensation he was left with a partner for some flirtation. He couldn't complain.

When the entanglement finally unwound, there was one enigma left to be solved, a mystery to decipher, one that brought on intricate controversies. Young Adib Barud, in charge of the store, still had not transformed it into the grandiose bazaar he had imagined and promised—he and Jamil before him—but he had straightened out the finances, reestablished its credit, and brought back its clientele. If the results had not been extraordinary, neither had they been bad. As far as was known, Adib never complained, always smiling and affable behind the counter, chatty and gossipy as only he could be. He'd learned his skills in the bar. The lady customers adored him.

In spite of being young, he took complete charge, a competent and hardworking boss, accepted and esteemed by his relatives. In addition to this, he was happy in his marriage. He showed himself to be a serene and faithful husband, charmed by the bed of his better half. He didn't get to be a singular example of monogamy, as Ibrahim had been in Sálua's time. Every so often he would accompany his father-in-law to have some fun at night with no set time for their return. On the occasion of her husband's first spree, Adma tried to go back to her old ways. She waited up, awake, gathering up wrath and venom. She turned into a viper and received him with sticks and stones, shrieks and sobs, a fine rowdy celebration. To begin the conversation Adib unloaded a potent pair of slaps on her, the prelude to a memorable thrashing, with which he made an example of her. He immediately mounted her with drive and devotion, leaving her finally calm and satisfied, purring. Whenever necessary and sometimes with no apparent need, he would repeat the treatment. That was how he tamed her, with beating and petting, in spite of being criticized by the male community and by a few ladies who held to the prevailing law—a citizen lies with his wife respectfully and for the purpose of making children in her, a sacred duty. For indecent things, dirty work, there are whores. Ibrahim's faithfulness was explained by his being the husband of Sálua, the most beautiful of beauties, a body well endowed with curves, ample flesh, the face of a proper woman, the eyes of a sultana. But how could one explain Adib's moderation? A hotheaded, husky fellow, formerly so welcomed by whores and concubines, he had become scarce and remote. What arts or artifices to keep him home at night were being used by Adma, an iron maiden, a dried codfish, an ironing board? When Adib ran his hand over her body on that unforgettable day of the donkey stampede, he discovered that was not the way she was. She had firm, sexy breasts. But was a good pair of tits enough to make up for all the rest? Or could Adma, perhaps, as some suggested and suspected in the heat of wild arguments, be one of those favored by God, who had awarded her the grace of a divine twat for a dick to dip into?

It was never known for sure. But Raduan Murad, as he recalled both the real and the magical limits of the story of Adma's nuptials, called his listeners' attention to the well-known circumstance that God is a Brazilian. Responsible for the future of Jamil Bichara, with that same efficiency he governed the fate of Adib Barud, both of them favored sons, both brought up with a love for business and money and with respect for the laws of southern Bahia. With the Muslim Allah using the bar boy to stop Jamil from running away from his destiny, Jehovah, the God of the Maronite Catholics, would do no less. He would not leave Adib in the lurch, stuck in a pile of shit. Adma hadn't inherited Sálua's facial features, her lovely body, but in recompense God had conceded her the best part of the inheritance, the principal part: that incomparable mystery that turns certain very rare women, pretty or ugly, irresistible. Sálua or Adma, it doesn't matter—one miracle less, one miracle more; miracles happened at the drop of a hat in those good times of the discovery of America by the Turks.

BAHIA, JULY; PARIS, OCTOBER; 1991

Postscript

At a certain time in Portugal, Jorge was writing a passage of *Showdown* in which he was telling about the marriage of Fadul Abdala, one of the heroes of the novel. I was quite taken with it. There were moments of great humor, and at the same time it was rather moving. One day I saw a huge pile of typewritten pages in the trash. I took a look and it was the whole chapter of the wedding. But Jorge, are you going to throw this away? He explained to me that it was too long—it was almost another novel inside the first one; the best place for it was the ash can. I couldn't convince him to keep the chapter, but I did save the originals in a folder. Years later, when the celebration of the fifth centenary of the discovery of America came along and knowing that I'd kept the original of that chapter, Jorge picked up the writing again and this book was born.

ZÉLIA GATTAI AMADO

Printed in the United States
by Baker & Taylor Publisher Services